BECAU

By

Willa Winters

Copyright © 2020

INTRODUCTION

I sure hope you all enjoy this pulsing hot erotica story of lust that knows no boundaries. Not race, not creed, not nationality will sway this horny chick from what she wants. And what she wants? Well in 1967, in the Deep South, it was still silently forbidden.

Yeah, Prudence Baker wanted black man Nathan Crawl from the moment she laid eyes on him. But her daddy, being the racist, white sheet wearing Grand Dragon pig he was, certainly was determined to keep those two apart.

But, like all true lust stories, their chemistry was not about to be denied!

And wait until you read the twist in this story!

Contents

LEGAL DISCLAIMER

Willa Winters Publishing

Because of Nathan
Copyright © 2020
All rights reserved.

No part of this book may be reproduced or transmitted in any form or by any means, electronic or mechanical, including photocopying, recording, or by information storage and retrieval system without the written permission of the author.

This book is a work of fiction. Any resemblance to actual persons, living or dead, events, or locations is purely coincidental. All rights reserved. Except as permitted, under the U.S. Copyright Act of 1976, no part of this publication may be reproduced, distributed, or transmitted in any form or by any means, or stored in a database or retrieval system, without the prior express, written consent of the author.

Violation of copyright, by domestic or foreign entities, is punishable by law, which may include imprisonment, a fine, or both.

This book is intended for mature audiences only.

PROLOGUE

My entire life I've always done what's been expected of me. Let me tell you that growing up in the South, in the heart of the Bible belt as a matter of fact, and the daughter of the town's bank president and acting mayor, you can well imagine that the expectations are quite extensive.

There's some hypocrisy at play here as well. It doesn't matter that our society is supposed to be all about equality, be it gender equality, or racial equality, or ethnic—it doesn't matter because for some reason, Branchville, Mississippi didn't get the memo on civil rights even after the years that have gone by since Title VII of the Civil Rights Act was passed.

Oh, people here *pretend* that there is no bigotry in Branchville—that this small little town is as liberated and politically correct as any northern *Yankee* city, but that's all window dressing. Things are calm and peaceful as long as the African American population here knows their place.

Yeah, I told you hypocrisy rules didn't I?

You might be surprised to know that many of the public figures, including city council members, ministers, bankers (my daddy, remember?) and lawyers here in Branchville have their white sheet garb ready in a moment's notice for whenever someone of the black race needs to be reminded of their place.

Yeah, it totally sucks. It is totally wrong. And I'm ashamed as hell of my bigoted ancestors, let me tell you!

And this is a white girl saying this, but for fuck's sake—what does it take for bigots to get a clue?

My best friend Velma and I have a bet going. I contend that Branchville will accept queers (the town's word, *not mine)* before they'll accept interracial relationships. Velma says it will be the other way around, but I don't think so. I mean my own father, a business and civic leader, remember? Well, all I can say is that he's one of the *worst*, and trust me, it pains me to admit that to anyone.

So, that is why I had to beg like hell and work my ass off to help with tuition, so that I could at least attend college somewhere other than around here. I attend Eastern Kentucky University, majoring in Economics. I will be going into my senior year next semester.

But at this minute?

Well, I'm currently home for the summer which means I work at the local pharmacy to help out with next semester's tuition. It's not a bad job. I cashier at the local Rexall that makes up one of the ten local businesses in the downtown area.

Little did I know that this summer would be one that I would never forget—or one that my father would never let me forget, after he discovered me in a *compromising* position at the annual Fourth of July Ice Cream Social at the local park.

And when I say compromising, let me tell you that is an *understatement.*

Being discovered, partially naked, in the deserted boathouse at the dock at Clearly Lake

with my beautiful black lover, Nathan Crawl,
licking melted chocolate ice cream out of my
pussy would be more exact.

Oh, and by the way? I was engaged at the
time to the preacher's son.

Here's how it all happened.

Chapter 1

June 5, 1967

I heard the little bell over the front door of the Rexall tinkle as I was putting a new roll of paper into my register. Seemed to me that Wally, the manager, ought to be thinking about getting one of those electronic registers that self-fed the roll of paper I grumbled to myself silently.

"Be with you in a second," I called out as whomever had entered the store was standing just on the other side of the checkout line, where all the candy and gum resided.

"Take your time," a deep, male voice said, "I ain't in no particular hurry."

I looked up and over the register quickly, and felt my heartbeat ramp up at the sight of what was surely one of the most gorgeous black men I'd ever set my eyes on.

Lordy sakes. He was tall, with broad shoulders that surely came from hard labor rather than some membership at a gym. His triceps bulged with corded muscles that seemed to ripple at the slightest movement as he tossed a couple of candy bars, a pack of gum, and a box of red hots onto the counter.

His dark skin was perfection in every way. He wore a white tee shirt that had the sleeves cut off, and clung to his torso like a second skin. His belly was firm and flat, and no doubt sported a six-pack. His work jeans were ripped in places, allowing me a peek at different spots of his well-muscled thighs.

My visual inventory of this gorgeous and virile black specimen was cut short when I heard him clear his throat.

"That's all I need, Miss," he said, his deep voice now had an even huskier tone to it. He'd caught me gawking at him!

Lordy! What he must think of me!

"Oh," I said with a blush, "I'm sorry, got a little distracted, I reckon," I blubbered like the idiot I apparently was. I rang him up quickly.

He handed me a ten, and when our hands touched, the rough feel of his dark skin actually sent an electric shock through my body, and I felt my dirty girl clench in response.

It was as if this man could read my body language and my mind. I heard him give me a soft chuckle and I handed him his change.

"You're new around here, aren't you?" I asked, as I pulled a small paper bag out and tossed his candy into it. "I haven't seen you around these parts before."

"Yes, ma'am," he drawled, his eyes now doing their damndest of taking physical inventory of me. "I'm with the crew that's in town laying the new pipe for the gas company. Gonna be here for a couple of months. The name's Nathan. Nathan Crawl."

I gave him a big Southern smile. Probably wasn't used to that being he was here in

Branchville, south of the Mason-Dixon Line for sure.

"Well Nathan Crawl," I cooed, "It's gonna be a pleasure seeing to your needs----I mean here at the Rexall," I finished, feeling my cheeks color with embarrassment.

What the ever loving fuck had gotten into me? I wasn't a flirt by nature, I swear! I had a fiancé for Chrissake! A nice *white boy* as my father called him, and the preacher's son at that! *'You can't do no better than that, Prudence.'*

And I could say without a moment's hesitation that Jeremy Wayne Gallendar would not appreciate it one little bit if he'd witnessed the way I was acting around Nathan Crawl. He was just as racist as everyone in this god-forsaken town that still thought and judged as if it were more than a hundred years ago! It just wasn't right. I hated where I lived, but I was stuck.

"I look forward to stopping in again, Miss----?"

I blushed again, realizing I hadn't properly introduced myself. Where had my manners gone? "I'm sorry, I'm Prudence Baker. My friends call me 'Pru'." I held out my hand for him to take, and my breath hitched just a little when he did. His hand was strong, warm and calloused because this man did hard work.

"It's very nice meeting you, Ms. Baker. I hope to see you again, soon. I'm off to the pond. Hear the fishing's good there."

I nodded and watched him as he turned and left the store. I let out an appreciative sigh, and then picked up one of the tabloids stacked near the register, and fanned my face and neck with it. It was hot here in Branchville, but I swear, when Nathan Crawl came in, the temp went up noticeably.

"What you looking at there, Pru?" Molly Jensen asked, coming up behind me. Molly was the late shift cashier. I hadn't realized my shift was nearly over so distracted I'd been over the past few minutes.

"Oh, one of the guys in town laying pipe for the gas company," I replied, still watching as he disappeared down the street. "He sure is a handsome specimen," I finished, still distracted.

"Hmm," she replied, putting her work smock on over her sun dress, "Looks to me like you're looking for trouble, Missy. Don't think you need anybody like him laying pipe around you."

I whirled around to face her. She had an ornery grin going on.

"Oh for Pete's sake, Molly," I snapped, moving out of the way so that she could take over. "Get your mind outta the gutter. I'm engaged. You know that. But *damn* . . . "

She shrugged. "Well, sure I know that. You know that. Jeremy Wayne knows that. But does your *dirty girl* know that?"

Her last comment didn't even deserve a response, so I didn't give her one as I counted my register, trying my best to ignore her taunting.

"You best be getting that black man out of your mind, girl. I'm all for a girl having her sexual freedom and sewing her own wild oats as long as she's still single, but don't go crossing racial lines. Not here. Not in this town that's for sure!"

I got my money counted, wrote it down on the daily sheet and gave Molly an eye roll. "Have a great shift, Molly. See you tomorrow," I said, grabbing my purse from behind the counter, and taking off into the June heat and humidity.

As I strolled down Main Street, towards our house at the edge of town, I decided to take the long way home. I wanted to walk down Pike Street where I knew they were laying the new gas lines. As I turned the corner, I saw the line of construction equipment sitting idle. It was after five o'clock. The crew was off for the day.

There was a trailer parked under one of the maple trees. That must be the construction office, but it appeared as deserted as everything else.

I continued walking, and took an even longer route when I turned on Pond Street and walked the three blocks to it.

The pond was at the edge of town, in the other direction from my house. It was more like a lagoon surrounded by a wooded area where it blessedly shielded the hot sun from penetrating the cool lapping water of the lagoon.

My daddy used to take me here after Mama died to feed the ducks and squirrels. It was quiet and peaceful. And at five-thirty on a weekday in June, it was mostly deserted. The kids in town went to the water park when it got this hot.

I walked down the dirt trail, and just around the bend I saw him.

Nathan Crawl.

His pole was bobbing in the dark water of the lagoon as he rested back against a log.

He didn't seem startled when I walked to where he was fishing, and plopped down next to him, tucking my bare legs up under me.

"Miss Baker," he said, his voice had a deep, rich tenor that drove me wild. "What brings you out in the heat of the late afternoon? Don't you have a nice air-conditioned home waiting for you?"

I wasn't sure what it was about Nathan Crawl that mesmerized me the way he did, but I knew I wanted to find out. There was this . . . this chemistry between us that was almost palpable.

My thighs squeezed together tightly, as I graced him with a smile. "You can drop the '*Miss*' Nathan, I ain't no Scarlett O'Hara here. I just thought maybe you being new around here, you might want some company. I know there's not a lot to do here in Branchville. It's a snoozer town."

"Among other things," he replied. "No bars, no clubs---that allow blacks in anyway. That's where the rest of the crew went after our shift was over. Some private club that Buck belongs to that don't particularly cater to the darker skinned as he put it. Since I'm the only black dude on the crew, well, let's just say I had to make alternate plans."

I sighed. "I know. It sucks, doesn't it? This place is Jerksville for sure. So behind the times. I want to apologize for that, Nathan. It really pisses me off. That's why I can hardly wait to finish college and get the hell outta this place. I go to college up north."

He cocked an eyebrow at me; his eyes were so damn dark they looked black. Like midnight. "Where's that?" he asked.

"Where's what?"

He laughed for the first time, and it was a deep, rich, throaty laugh that was so damn sexy and contagious, that I joined in.

"You must think I'm a real ditz, I swear. I'm really not, I promise. I go to Eastern Kentucky."

"And you call that, *north*?" he asked, his eyes danced with humor.

"Well," I replied with a drawl, "It's way north of here. And to be honest, it's like another planet there, Nathan. I hate the thought of being stuck here forever."

His brow furrowed in confusion. "Why do you feel you'll be stuck here, girl? You're in college, you've got choices, right?"

I shook my head. "Not really. I'm engaged to the preacher's son. He's tied to the community---that's the way he puts it. He doesn't want to leave. But it's non-negotiable if he actually wants to tie the knot with this girl. I just haven't given him that ultimatum just yet."

Nathan pulled his pole from the water and placed it on the grass beside him. He turned his body to face me; his large hands rested on his jean clad knees.

"Now that doesn't make a whole lot of sense, Prudence. Sounds to me like you may want to re-think that whole engagement thing."

"Please, call me Pru? And you're right. I've got no business staying engaged to Jeremy Wayne. But it's kind of expected."

"Expected? As in arranged?"

"Well, in a way, I suppose."

I wasn't prepared for the low, guttural growl that escaped his full lips. "Only white folks," he said, shaking his head, and grunting out a sarcastic laugh. "When will people down here get with the program? Girl, you're too young and beautiful to promise your life to someone who obviously won't make you happy."

"I know," I sighed, "But for now? Well, for now I'm still single. I still can make my own choices and decisions. And in case you haven't noticed, I chose to be here, Nathan."

The silence was almost palpable between us. He raised a hand to brush the perspiration from his forehead and glanced around.

"What is it you want from me, Pru?" he asked hoarsely. "I'm not looking to get lynched, you know?"

"Oh stop," I said with a laugh. "We aren't that *far* behind. Are you married, Nathan?" I asked succinctly.

"No, ma'am."

"Good. If I can be totally honest with you, I'm kind of drawn to you. And I know that sounds odd being that we just met a couple of hours ago. But there's well . . . there's something about you that sparks something in me. It's hard to explain."

"Try," he challenged, his eyes raking over me.

"Okay, so I'm looking to see how a black cock feels if you want to know the truth. You fascinated me from the first second I laid eyes on you. I hope---well, I hope I haven't offended you."

He took a moment before responding to me, and I held a breath, hoping like hell he wasn't going to tell me to get lost. But it was the truth I'd given him, no matter how weird or crazy it sounded, there was something that pulsed within me that wanted to see how it felt to have his big black cock filling the walls of my pussy.

I'd grown wet for him in those few brief seconds before he responded.

"Where?" he asked. "Where can we go so nobody sees this black dude fucking your pearly white pussy?"

My pulse quickened and I smiled, knowing that shit was about to get real.

CHAPTER 2

The deserted boat house on the other side of the lagoon was hidden by a thick cluster of overgrown evergreen and oleander bushes.

If Nathan was skeptical of my motives, he hadn't shown it on the short trek over here. I pushed open the splintered wooden door, and stepped inside, waiting for him to follow.

Once inside, I closed the door behind us, and flipped the iron latch to keep it locked from potential intruders, although there'd been nobody around at all.

The wooden structure was old and rickety; cracked boards here and there allowed for streams of sunlight to filter through, casting enough light to show the layers of dust on the stained wooden benches that were built into the structure, and the cobwebs dangling from the overhead beams.

It smelled musty, and the heat of the day had blessedly been kept somewhat at bay because of the boarded up windows.

Nathan's gaze was on me now, his eyes perusing my bare legs, my cotton sundress didn't do much to hide my own curves, and my hard nipples now strained against the cloth with his nearness to me.

There was something exquisite about the manly scent of this man. He smelled of soap and his skin sported a thin film of perspiration that was heady to me. It was totally chemistry. His hormones were my own personal aphrodisiac.

And Nathan knew it.

"Is this what you want, little girl? A big black cock inside that pretty pussy of yours?" Nathan asked, his voice so low it was almost a growl.

I reckoned the sound of his manly voice talking vulgar to me was the reason I started to cream down my thighs, my dirty girl clenching in anticipation for the filling I was about to get.

"Yes, sir. I wanna know what all the fuss is about. See if you can fuck better than a white, country boy."

Not that I had much experience with that, but he didn't need to know my whole sexual history. Our time was going to be better spent I could tell.

"Sit up on that table over there and show me your cunt, Miss Pru. You won't getting my dick until I've licked every drop of what I'm guessing is a very wet pussy."

I did as he asked, hopping on the table, spreading my thighs and lifting up my sundress so I was completely bare to this man I knew next to nothing about.

All I knew was that for some inexplicable reason he fascinated me. I'd never had a black man inside of me, but I'd always been curious.

Back in high school, Lilly Mantel had gone out with a black guy from Siler City, the next town over. Her parents had had a royal fit about it, but she hadn't cared one bit.

She said he had the biggest cock she'd ever seen, and Lilly Mantel was pure slut. That was a fact. If anyone had felt their share of cocks, it would have been that girl.

Well, she ended up getting pregnant her junior year of high school. Her parents threw her out of the house and she ended up over in Siler City with her black boyfriend and a trailer full of biracial youngins last I heard. Word had it that she was happy though. The cock must have been worth it I decided.

I looked up at Nathan Crawl. Damned if he wasn't beautiful and sexy as all get out. Mostly, I knew I wanted to be his fuck doll.

"So pretty. Is your cunt lonely, Pru Baker?" He asked, absentmindedly as his large dark finger ran a line from my ass to my clit, slowly and deliberately. I saw his tongue flicker over his bottom lip.

I whimpered, and wriggled my butt against the rough wooden table. I needed more than what he was giving me. I tilted my head back, closing my eyes. "Yes, sir."

"Call me 'sir' one more time and I won't get any foreplay done. I'll fuck the sense right out of you and then fuck you again for good measure," he said, taking a step closer to where I needed him.

I opened my eyes and stared right at him. "Yes, sir." I was taunting him because I didn't need soft and romantic. I didn't need foreplay.

I wanted rough and demanding. I craved to see a man lose control for the sole purpose of fucking the sense right out of me.

"Good answer," he murmured as he popped off the button of his jeans, slid the zipper down and freed the anaconda that was his cock.

Holy mother of all that was sin! My eyes widened at the scene, my mouth parted with the knowledge that I was about to get impaled by the massive dick before me.

I may have had an orgasm on the spot. God he was gorgeous in every way. And his cock? Well, his cock was what every woman dreamed off I was sure. I felt myself hesitate because of his girth.

"Don't worry, little girl. It'll fit."

I'd taken Sex-Ed classes. I knew anything could fit in my pussy if lubed up enough. That wasn't the reason for my reaction. I just couldn't wait to experience it. Now.

Spreading my legs wider, I brought my finger to my cunt and stuck a finger inside, getting myself nice and wet for his massive dick.

"No foreplay needed. Rip me apart, if you want. If you can. I want to be able to rethink of this exact moment while I'm getting myself off, in two, ten or twenty years. I have no doubt, Nathan, that you will be the best fuck of my life. You ever fucked a white girl before, Nathan?"

His gaze on me was serious and intent. A look of pure lust crossed over his face. "Can't say that I have, but there's always a first, and I'm willing and able as you can see."

No sooner had his words landed on my ears, then Nathan had his hands on my thighs and his dick poking at my slick entrance.

"Condom!" I quickly blurted out. I wasn't on the pill and God forbid I got pregnant. It wasn't like I was having sex with my fiancé and even in the Bible Belt, we didn't quite believe in the Immaculate Conception.

"Don't have one. Wasn't exactly expecting this, you know?"

I grinned at his immediate retreat, seeing the precum oozing from the head of his dick as he did so.

"Good thing I'm a good girl scout," I said with a sly grin, reaching for my purse and taking out a foil packet. Extra large for her pleasure.

Yeah, I anticipated his size. I'd pocketed these from the drug store while Molly was in the restroom. "I came prepared Sir Nathan."

Nathan visibly relaxed, knowing he was about to get lucky after all.

I tossed him the packet and watched, mesmerized as he slid the condom down his smooth black length and then zeroed in on me.

"Ready to scream, little girl?" He asked, piercing me with his hungry stare.

"Yes, sir."

In one quick step, Nathan had one hand in my hair, the other on my hip and his dick buried deep inside my pussy.

"Holy shit, you have the tightest cunt I've ever felt. Good God, girl. How I am supposed to walk away from Heaven?"

I don't know why his words warmed my heart, but they did. I wanted to feel this cherished for the rest of my life, all the while being fucked like the slut I knew I'd be treated like if anyone found out what I was doing at that moment.

"Harder, Nathan. Please." I begged, as he brought his mouth to mine and invaded my senses from cunt to mouth.

His hips pistoned, in and out, with carnal urgency as the hand he'd had on my hip slid over between our bodies and circled my clit. I was two seconds from falling apart. From coming all over his dick.

"That's right, little girl. Squeeze that cunt of yours nice and tight around my dick. Do it. Hell yeah!"

In those moments of total bliss, I felt like a queen. I also felt like a whore. I loved it in equal measure.

Nathan pulled on my hair, forcing my head to fall back. His mouth latched on to my nipple and sucked it inside as his tongue flicked it mercilessly.

"I'm gonna come, Nathan. Oh my God, I'm gonna..." I did as promised. My pussy convulsed, my muscles squeezing my to high heaven and my voice echoed around the walls of the beaten down cabin.

Soon after, I heard Nathan's groan as he emptied himself inside the condom, his fingers painfully curling around my hair.

Before we could catch our breaths, the door to the cabin burst open from the hinges with a brutal force. Lord Almighty! My worst nightmare came to life!

My daddy was staring at a picture he could have never imagined in his wildest dreams.

His little girl impaled by a big black man, her face flushed from the extraordinary orgasm she had just been gifted.

I was fucked.

(And not in a good way.)

CHAPTER 3

I was talking to Velma on the phone in my bedroom. Daddy had gone to work, and the house was empty with the exception of Charlotte, our housekeeper and me.

"So, what happened then?" she asked excitedly.

"Oh God, it was so horrible," I told her. "I thought Daddy was going to kill the both of us! If he'd had his shotgun with him, I'm not so sure he wouldn't have. He hollered for me to pull my dress down, and warned Nathan that if he saw his black ass in town ever again he'd take a whip to him and get away with it!"

"No he didn't," she rasped, clearly shocked. "Did Nathan run outta there?"

I smiled reflecting back on that horrible moment. "Actually, he acted totally unaffected. He pulled his dick out of me and it was still glistening with our juices on it. He took his time, pulling up his jeans and fastening them up. He never said a word to Daddy. He shrugged, tossed me a wink and left the boat house."

"Are you serious?" she asked, totally enthralled with my re-telling of what had happened. "So what did your daddy say to you?"

"He told me that what I'd done was unacceptable. He'd come looking for me because some nosy old lady had spotted us going in there and called him. She thought I'd been forced into that boat house. Yeah right!"

We both giggled at that notion.

"Anyway, he said if he ever caught me with a black guy again, I was out of the house for good. You know what?"

"What?"

"I don't give a damn, Velma. Those few minutes with Nathan in that damn boat house were the best ever. I only hope he didn't take Daddy's threat to heart."

I heard Velma sigh from her end. "Well, what are you going to do?" she asked.

"I need your help, Vel. Daddy has everyone in town keeping an eye out on me. He gave them some stupid story about me having a stalker. I can't go risk going down to Pike Street. Can you take a message to him for me, please?"

There was a pause on the other end. "Well . . . I don't want Bruce getting word I was down where all those guys are laying pipe," she said.

"Listen," I said, "just give him my private phone number. Tell him to call me, that's all you have to do. I promise it will just take a second. Please?"

"Okkay," she finally relented, "But Pru, are you sure you know what you're doing here? If Jeremy Wayne ever gets wind of this---"

"Fuck that white boy! He's out of town for another four weeks. Besides that, he doesn't know how to fuck me the way I wanna be fucked. I need Nathan again. I swear I need that black cock inside of me again. It's driving me nuts."

"How in the hell are you gonna manage that?" she asked.

"Big house here. My room's on the other side of the house. Daddy has no way of knowing who sneaks in and out through my bedroom window. Jeremy's done it enough, trust me."

We ended the call with Velma promising she'd make a trip downtown to give Nathan the message before five. I needed him here tonight.

I took a bubble bath, piling my long dark curls on top of my head. I ran the sponge all over my body, my eyes closed, remembering how his hands, his lips and his tongue had felt as they traveled all over my creamy white skin.

I wanted him in my bed. I wanted to see how our bodies looked connected: dark skin flush against white skin. I bet it was a beautiful sight.

At a little after five, Charlotte tapped on my bedroom door. "Prudence," she called out, "I'm getting ready to leave for the day, child. Do you need anything?"

"No, Charlotte. I'm good. Thanks."

"Well, alright then. There's some cold chicken and potato salad in the fridge if you get hungry. Your daddy has a town meeting so he won't be home until eight-thirty or nine."

"Thanks, Charlotte. See you tomorrow," I replied just as the phone on my nightstand rang.

I jumped across my bed to answer it. My heart raced as the deep, manly voice resonated in my ear.

"It's Nathan, got your message, Ms. Baker."

"Don't you think we know one another enough for you to cal me Pru?" I teased.

There was dead silence.

I sighed. "I need you to come over, Nathan. I feel like we didn't finish what we started the other day."

I heard him release a hard sigh from the other end of the phone. "Are you fixing to get me shot, little girl?"

His tone almost sounded amused. "Daddy's not here. Won't be home until later this evening. I need you to fuck me."

He let go of a soft, deep chuckle. "Like the black dick do you?"

My pussy pulsed at his words. "I've got a craving for it, I admit. I'd like to taste it, unless of course, you have an objection to that? I'd like to run my tongue very slowly along the length of it, and then suck the cockhead and watch it grow. Then maybe deep throat it and suck it until my throat is coated with your precum."

I heard a manly growl from the other end and I smiled, knowing that I'd definitely piqued his interest. "Is your big black dick hard thinking about what I want to do to it, Nathan? I crooned.

"Give me directions, Pru," he said in a husky growl.

I gave him the address, along with directions to my bedroom window. There were shrubs that hid my room from street view, so I assured him he'd have no worries about nosey neighbors around here. But I warned him to wait until it was dark out before coming around.

The last thing he said to me was, "This time, no condoms, white girl. I want you to feel my skin against the inside of your pink, juicy cunt. I want you to feel every fucking drop of my cum when I get off inside of you, and when it drips back out of your pussy hours later, do you hear?"

I felt my pussy clench and dampen with his sexy words.

"Answer me," he demanded.

"Yes, Nathan. I understand. Whatever you say."

"I say get ready for the dark ride tonight, Ms. Prudence."

CHAPTER 4

It was a bit after ten o'clock when I heard the soft tapping at my bedroom window at the side of the house. I was wearing only a silk shift. I hadn't even bothered with panties, knowing they'd only be ripped off within minutes of Nathan getting inside my room.

I hurried over to the window and pushed the curtains aside raising the sash in an instant. Nathan only took seconds to hoist his large, muscular body through the window, landing on his feet just inches from me.

I gazed up at him, already mesmerized by his size, his closeness, and the heady scent of male testosterone that seemed to be seeping from every pore of his dark chocolate skin. He was wearing a black wife beater tee, and dark khaki pants.

My hand reached up to trace one of the corded muscles that bulged from his triceps, but his large hand quickly brushed me away. He turned and closed the curtains.

"We're not puttin' a show on here little girl," he growled. "You got lights on in here, and I don't give a damn how secluded your bedroom window is, there's still people out and about on a night this hot and humid."

I smirked, and now that the curtains were closed, resumed fondling his muscular body with my hand, letting it glide slowly over his damp, dark skin.

"Mmm, well aren't you glad to come in outta the heat then, Nathan?" I teased coyly. "We've got our AC going full blast for your comfort."

He remained silent, toeing off his shoes and I watched as he padded over to my bedroom door to make sure it was securely locked. When he stooped down and lifted the pink dust ruffle on my bed, I couldn't help but giggle.

"And what exactly are you looking for?" I asked, "Or is it just paranoia?"

He got back up, and pulled his shirt up and over his head. "Got reason to be. Don't want any unexpected visitors busting in this time. Had to make sure you weren't setting me up."

I walked over to where he was unfastening his belt and I frowned as I gazed up at his eyes. "And why would I do that since I flat out told you I had a craving for your cock?"

He scoffed, as he pulled the belt off and dropped it to the carpeted floor. "Why mine?" he asked, unbuttoning his fly where my eyes quickly widened at the growing bulge in his crotch.

"Because I loved the way it felt . . . you know, when you were fucking me the other day. You hit some very sweet spots. It made me want more," I replied sincerely.

"So, white girl loves black cock, is that about right? Don't the white boys do it for you?"

I cocked my head, and let my tongue flicker across my bottom lip seductively. "Not quite as well as you," I replied.

And then I dropped down to my knees in front of him. My hand brushed his away from where he'd been unfastening his fly.

I finished the job.

As his big, rigid cock sprang free, it slapped against his abdomen. "Damn bitch," he sighed, "You've got me hard as a fucking rock just thinking about that tight white pussy of yours. Mmm."

My hand grasped his dick, but his girth was such that I couldn't completely close my fingers around it. I lowered my lips to it, and slowly and leisurely ran my tongue up and down the full length of it.

Nathan groaned as my tongue darted into the slit, capturing the clear beads of precum that had gathered there. I lapped them up, twirling my tongue in a circular motion around the head of his cock. He groaned again, his hands now fisting my hair. "That's it baby, suck my cock like your life depends on it, hear?"

I nodded, and opened my mouth, drawing him inside, and trying like hell to fight my gag reflex at the size of his dick. I failed. I gagged.

"Is it too big for you, baby?" Nathan soothed.

I released his cock, and allowed my hand to jack it for a moment while I swallowed the saliva that had gathered at the back of my throat. "Oh no, I'm good. I can handle you, Nathan."

He chuckled softly as I once again took possession of his cock in my mouth.

My hands gently massaged his balls, and I loved it that he was rocking back on his heels, his hands once again gripping my head as he rocked into me. "God damn, girl. You gonna make me lose my load. We can't have that now can we?"

But I was on a mission. I wanted to show Nathan Crawl that I could not only blow his cock, but I could blow his mind as well with my sexual expertise.

His body was exquisite in every way. His balls were full and firm, loaded with his magic seed that I wanted inside of me. He tasted better than any other guy I'd blown before.

I moaned as he continued to thrust in and out of my mouth, the head of his dick rubbing against my tonsils, but I didn't gag; I didn't flinch. As far as I was concerned, he could shoot his big load down my throat and I would swallow every damn drop of it. I knew as virile as Nathan was, he'd have more ready and waiting to spill into my pussy in a matter of minutes.

But, Nathan had other plans it seemed. He pulled his dick from my mouth, and quickly removed his pants. In a flash, he pulled me up from where I'd been kneeling, and pulled my silk nightie up and over my head.

"What?" I started, but he was a man on a mission, and I shivered at the intensity with which he was executing that mission.

"I told you I wanted to come inside that pussy, and that's exactly what I'm gonna do."

And I knew I needed to press him to use a condom, and that he wasn't going to be pleased. "I've . . . I've got condoms in the drawer next to the bed," I squeaked as he picked me up and walked the few steps over to my bed.

He laid me face up on my bed, and my eyes caught the side of his glistening hard dick, as he kneed my thighs apart, one of his large hands grasping his erection as he guided it towards my hungry pussy.

"As I've already said there'll be no rubbers. I want to feel your juicy pussy against the skin of my dick. Now are we doing this or not?" he asked, the head of his cock barely touching my hole.

I bit my lower lip with uncertainty. "What . . . what if you get me pregnant?" I whined.

"That's a chance you'll have to take. I can't make any promises little girl."

This was torture.

Pure torture.

But I knew in the end my hunger for lust would win out over my better judgment. "Fuck me, Nathan," I mewled. "Fuck me good with that big, black cock of yours."

And with that, Nathan thrust his cock into me, grunting with the effort. His hands were now braced on either side of me, palm side down, as he rocked in and out of me with delicious precision and prowess.

"Mmm," I moaned with every thrust he pushed into me. My legs wrapped around his hips, and as he continued pummeling me with his rock hard cock, my toes dug into his muscular ass cheeks, and my mind was devoid of anything other than the pleasure he was giving me.

His head dipped down, and his lips found mine, his tongue plunging inside with a hunger that nearly sucked the breath out of me. My tongue explored his mouth, and I loved his taste there too.

"You like the way I fuck you, Pru?" he asked, his tongue now tracing a path along my jaw as I bucked up against him, mewling like a hungry kitten.

"God, yes," I rasped, "Don't stop. Please, Nathan, keep fucking me good and proper," I moaned, my fingernails raking a path down his well muscled back.

He thrust into me even deeper, his arm drawing my legs up higher so that he could bury himself inside of me to the hilt.

He moaned at the tightness of our connection, his hips swiveled, allowing the head of his cock to hit that magic spot deep inside of me.

"Oh God! Right there! That's it!"

"You like that spot little girl?" he asked, his warm breath caressing my ear, causing me to shiver with pleasure.

"I'm getting ready to come," I mewled, arching my back and pushing my pelvis up against him.

My swollen clit was now rubbing against his abdomen, and the wet sounds of our damp skin slapping skin was a testament to just how sexually charged our bodies were as we mated.

I gazed down at the meshing of his black skin against my pearly white, and it was a beautiful sight. I strained to watch his cock as it pistoned in and out of me, and my last shreds of self-control were gone as my orgasm took over.

I moaned and squealed my pleasure as Nathan pounded into me, his husky moans telling me he was coming too.

"You ready for my seed, Ms. Pru? Nathan's gonna come and squirt it all inside that tight pussy of yours. You ready to take it?"

"Yes," I said, my orgasm now peaking, "Give it to me," I sobbed, "I'm ready to take it all."

And with a hearty grunt, Nathan pumped into me with a vengeance and then stilled. His eyes were squeezed shut, and he let out an almost feral groan as I felt his dick throb inside of me, followed by the warm, jet stream of his cum as he filled me up with his powerful seed.

Over and over again I could feel the spurts of his cum as his balls emptied themselves inside of me.

Finally, he collapsed down next to me, throwing his forearm up and over his brow, and exhaling a deep breath. "Fuck girl, I'm spent," he said with a sexy growl. "You done took it all and then some."

I giggled and rolled over so that I was lying across his expansive chest. "And just think, in ten or fifteen minutes, we'll be good to go again, right?"

He cocked a brow and gazed down at me, his nostrils flared with his need to mate with me again. As much as I loved the feel of Nathan Crawl fucking me, I knew damn well he enjoyed it every bit as much.

"Damn girl. You gonna wear my black ass out, aren't you?"

"I'd like to try," I replied, "You know what they say---what doesn't kill you only makes you stronger."

CHAPTER 5

Two days later, I was working my shift at the Rexall Drug Store when Velma popped in for a chat. We'd talked on the phone the day after Nathan had come to my house.

Of course, being best friends, Velma and I had no secrets from one another. I'd thoroughly enjoyed giving her a detailed replay of everything that had transpired between Nathan and me the night before. Well, not really the night before, because he'd stayed all through the night, fucking me in every position imaginable--- and some that were not.

"Oh no he didn't!" she squealed when I told her how Nathan had lowered my pussy down onto his face and licked the dripping cum from it as it dribbled down onto his chin.

"He surely did," I maintained, "And I sucked him off after he fucked me and tasted myself on his cock!"

"Noooo," she said, and I knew without even seeing her that her eyes were as wide as kid at Christmas. "So, how did it . . . taste?" she asked reluctantly.

"Um . . . well, kinda like tuna," I replied with a giggle. "Nathan even calls it *tuna diving*."

We both had broken into a fit of laughter with that one.

So, when Velma came bouncing into the drug store right before my lunch break, I was delighted to see my best friend in person.

"Hey girl," I said, closing out my register so Molly could take over while I went to lunch, "What brings you into town?"

She shrugged. "I was bored. It's my day off. Thought maybe we could have lunch?"

"Sure thing," I said, giving her a smile and grabbing my purse from under the counter. "Be back in an hour," I called over to Molly. "Where you wanna go?" I asked Velma as we headed out the door.

"How about the Tastee Freeze over on Pike," she suggested, "It's two for one foot long day."

I slowed my steps to a halt. Velma didn't realize it until she'd walked a couple yards ahead of me. She finally turned to see what was holding me up. "What?" she asked, her forehead wrinkled in confusion, "You don't want to go there?"

I started walking toward her, "Velma," I hissed, "That's where the construction crew is laying pipe, remember?"

"Yeah. So? I thought maybe you'd like to run into Nathan. Maybe give him a sexy shake of your tail feathers?" she teased.

"You know if I'm seen anywhere near Nathan, I'm dead white meat. Daddy has people watching me. I just can't take the chance."

She frowned and chewed thoughtfully on her bottom lip. Velma was a sweetheart. She really was. With her fiery red hair, and her cute freckle-splattered face, she looked like a fifteen year-old instead of a nineteen-year old same as me.

"You know, that just really sucks," she remarked. "How about this. You stay at the gazebo in the center of town, and I'll go get our foot longs and bring them back. We can eat in the shade at the gazebo, how's that?"

I nodded, "That'll work, I reckon. Hey, if you see Nathan, can you give him a message for me? Daddy's back home and breathing down my neck as usual. I'm afraid to even get on my private line. I need to see Nathan again."

"Okay, so what do you want me to tell him?"

I tapped my foot. "I'm thinking," I replied. "Okay, have him to meet me this evening, say around nine o'clock at the log where he fishes."

"You want him to meet you at a . . . *log*?" she asked, her eyes widening. "Like right out in the open?"

"It'll be getting dark by then, and besides, where that log is, it's pretty secluded. Lots of bushes and trees. Besides that, Daddy will think I'm in my room. I'm gonna sneak out my window."

"Okay," she said with a sigh. "I'll let him know."

"Thanks," I said with a smile, "Now scoot. I'm starving just thinking about how much he's gonna wear my ass and pussy out tonight!"

When Velma got back to the gazebo with our food, she immediately told me that my message had been delivered.

"He's gonna be there, right?" I asked, taking a sip of my chocolate milkshake.

She nodded, taking a huge bite out of her foot long Coney, "But he said to make it ten o'clock instead of nine. Said it'll be darker by then."

"Oh. Okay," I said, feeling a tinge of disappointment that I'd have to wait an extra hour for Nathan to sink his bold black cock into me, but it was worth the wait I suppose.

The rest of the afternoon seemed to drag on once I knew what would be in store for me tonight. I tried my best to keep busy, but every five or ten minutes I was glancing up at the clock. Molly noticed.

"What you keep looking at that clock for, Pru? Got big plans after work? Don't tell me Jeremy Wayne is coming home this evening?"

"Oh. No. He's still out of town. I'm just looking forward to going home, taking me a bubble bath, doing my nails, watching a good movie on television."

"Hmmph," she said, wiping off her counter with a damp cloth, "Don't seem like anything all that special."

"Well . . . uh, I'm hoping to hear from Jeremy, you know? He tries to call me collect a couple of nights a week. He's about due, that's all."

"I see," she replied, her tone told me she wasn't buying it.

Oh well. I didn't care. I didn't answer to Molly, or to anyone else around this hick town that was still full of bigots and judgmental people. It was one reason why I'd decided to select a college up north. It didn't take long for the self-righteous, hypocritical residents of

Branchville to get on my freaking nerves, and that included my daddy!

Finally, five o'clock rolled around and my shift was blessedly over. I clocked out and started for home, stopping at Woolworth's to buy some sexy black lace panties and a matching push-up bra. I'd wear these tonight, under one of my summer shifts for when I met Nathan at the pond.

I giggled softly thinking about how he'd likely rip them off of me in his need to possess my body with his. His dick; my cunt. It was if they were almost magnetically drawn to one another.

CHAPTER 6

Once I got home, Charlotte fussed at me until I sat down and ate the supper she'd prepared for me and Daddy. Roast pork, mashed potatoes and gravy, and carrots. If Charlotte had her way, I'd pack twenty pounds on in no time.

She was always fussing and nagging about me being too skinny, and men liking some meat on the bones.

"What are your plans for this evening, Prudence," Daddy asked, shoveling a forkful of mashed potatoes into his mouth.

I shrugged. Daddy knew that I was still feeling salty about the way he'd threatened me after catching me with Nathan. "Not much. Taking a bath, doing my nails. Not much else to do."

"Have you heard from Jeremy Wayne?" he asked, wiping his mouth with the linen napkin.

"Not for a few days. Maybe he'll call tonight. I don't know," I replied.

"He's a fine man, Prudence. You'd do well to show him he's worth a damn and get your head outta---"

"More roast, Mayor Baker," Charlotte interrupted bringing another platter of the meat out from the kitchen.

"May I be excused Daddy?" I piped up, scooting my chair away from the table, "I'm full."

"I have a freshly baked apple pie for dessert," Charlotte replied, "You love my pies, Prudence."

"I surely do, Charlotte. Maybe later?"

"You're excused," my father replied testily.

I escaped to my room, happy to be out from under my daddy's watchful eye. I knew he'd be in his room and likely asleep by nine o'clock what with the heavy meal Charlotte prepared for him this evening.

I took a leisurely bubble bath, and then did my nails just as planned. I kept my television on, catching a glimpse of this or that while I prepared myself for my date later with Nathan.

Date?

Who was I kidding? This was nothing close to a date. It was more like an appointment to fornicate right out in the open, under a star-studded night sky.

It was kind of romantic--at least that part of it I decided.

Damn it! I'd grown damp just anticipating Nathan and me fucking under the night stars. I glanced at the clock on my dresser. It was only ten minutes after nine. But I didn't care. It was dark enough out. Besides that, it would take me fifteen minutes to walk there, so it was one way to kill time.

Maybe Nathan would show early anyway. Maybe he was just as anxious for our coupling as I was. I smiled at the notion.

I tossed a light cotton red shift over my new black lace underwear, and slid my feet into a pair of tennis shoes, and silently exited my room through the window.

The darkness wasn't quite at full form yet, but it was getting close. The night was going to be lit by a full moon, which I was thankful for to help visibility in the shadowy darkness.

The air was thick with humidity, but a soft breeze was kicking up which made it more bearable. I was spoiled with our house having central air and all. I loved the sounds of the crickets chirping in unison like a cheerful church choir. The fireflies glowed off and on as I made my way towards the park where the fishing pond was located.

The streets of Branchville were deserted as usual. This was definitely a small town that pulled their sidewalks in before nightfall no matter what time of year.

I made my way silently into the deserted park, and headed over towards the thicket of pine and evergreen trees that lined the area just north of the pond.

I was about ten or twelve yards from the edge of the pond, near where the big log was located when I suddenly heard something that caused me to stop dead in my tracks.

My heart was pounding, and I strained to make out the sounds I was hearing. It was familiar - yet not familiar for all the sense that made. I held my breath as if that would help the clarity of the noises that floated effortlessly to my ears.

Muffled sounds.

Grunts and groans. Masculine sounding. And then a shrill whimper. And then another. It was hard to distinguish whether the whimpers were those of pleasure or pain--at first.

And then the realization hit me square in the face as I recognized the sounds of fucking. Not only that, but I knew it was Nathan by the deep, throaty growls and grunts.

"You like me pounding into that red-haired pussy of yours, girl?" he asked, his voice husky with lust. "You squeezing it like you're ready for me to come inside of you."

"Not yet, Nathan, please? I want more," Velma's quivering voice, cut through the darkness as I moved slowly towards the log.

As I moved into the clearing where the huge log was resting on the banks of the pond, the full moon cast its glow on the lapping water of the pond, causing a reflective light that served to illuminate the area, allowing me a bird's eye view of my best friend being fucked by my black man!

CHAPTER 7

I was livid at watching Velma, her back to me, as she moved up and down on Nathan's big cock.

She swiveled her full, rounded hips down on him, leaning forward so that her clit was rubbing against his abdomen. I knew exactly how that felt. I had even described in great detail how I had ridden Nathan's cock the same way she was right at this moment.

"Mmm, oh you feel so damn good, Nate," she gasped, as her momentum picked up. "Pru was right about your cock. I know I'm not going to be able to last much longer," she rasped.

I watched as Nathan's large black hands braced on either side of her hips, as he rolled them so that she was in sync with his thrusting from beneath her. He groaned again, pressing her ass tighter against him as he increased the tempo.

I wasn't going to stand by and watch this for one second longer! Before I could even think about it, I marched up to where they were, and shoved Velma with all of my strength, knocking her to the side, where her cunt released Nathan's cock, and she fell to the ground, landing with a loud "Oomph" on her ass.

"What the fuck!" Nathan yelled, his still erect dick dancing around as if searching for a wet pussy to bury itself into. I had just the one.

"You! You're fucking my best friend!" I accused, pulling my shift up over my head, and toeing off my sneakers.

"Hey girl, she said you weren't showing."

His eyes flickered over me, resting on my fancy black lace underwear, as he licked his bottom lip. "Red said she'd be glad to fill in . . . now what you think you're doing coming up on us and pushing the bitch off my cock?"

I turned to where Velma was getting up from the grass, rubbing her backside. I was speechless.

"I'll take care of you in a bit," Nathan snapped, giving me a hateful glare. "Near as I can tell, nobody owns me, despite the fact we're south of the Mason-Dixon Line. Now you, Prudence," he continued, the anger still very much evident in his voice, "You have a choice. You can stay, as long as you keep your mouth shut, and wait your turn. Or, if you find that too difficult, then you can just high tail your uppity white ass out of here. Either way, I'm gonna finish what I started here with Red. It's your decision, but make it now cause I'm fixing to fuck her, and if you interrupt us again, I'll personally haul your ass outta here."

I was not only speechless; I was totally dumbfounded at Nathan's audacity, and even more so that my best friend had betrayed me like that.

Velma slinked by me, whispering a soft, "I'm sorry, Pru. I . . . I just couldn't help it." But that did little to appease my rising anger.

I wanted to walk away as if neither one of them were worth my time or my anger. I knew that I should put my pride ahead of any of this, walk away with my head held high. But that would have been too damn difficult to pull off and I knew it. I would be the odd girl out. I would be the one going without.

Fuck that!

I crossed my legs and lowered myself down to the soft grass, and bit my tongue to keep from verbally lashing out at the both of them. I needed to keep my mouth shut like Nathan had warned, because I had no doubt he would follow through on his threat if I didn't.

Nathan took Velma by the hand as she crept back over to him, and pulled her naked body up against his in a passionate kiss---for my benefit, I was sure of that.

So, Nathan enjoyed the jealous bit that I'd played. I watched as his large hands dropped down to her ass, and he greedily messaged her cheeks, grinding his semi-erect dick against her crotch.

She moaned and writhed against him, their kissing getting more and more urgent and passionate. Nathan fisted her red ponytail, twisting her head back so that he could plant frenzied kisses on her neck and collarbone.

"I'm getting hard for you, Red," he said, "Your pussy getting wet for me?"

She nodded, and I watched as one of Nathan's hands snaked around, his fingers plunging inside of her cunt as she groaned and humped against him with lust and desire.

"Ah yeah. Nice and wet. That's my girl," he cooed, his mouth now capturing hers again. "C'mon. Big Nate wants to pump his big dick into your slick pussy. This time, I'm driving," he indicated, lowering her down to the soft grass next to the log.

She stretched out before him, and momentarily her green eyes locked with my angry ones, but she looked away quickly. Her tongue flickered across her lower lip as she gazed up at Nathan, whose huge thighs were now spread wider so that they were braced on either side of her torso. They were like massive tree trunks.

His right hand guided his huge erection towards her, and as he lowered himself and entered her, I caught her audible gasp as he filled her cunt with himself.

"Mmm," he moaned, "Nice and tight. Just the way I like my pussy," he remarked as he started a slow, methodical thrusting within her. "You doing okay?" he asked.

"Oh yes," she crooned, "You feel so damn good."

"Alright then. I'm going to start fucking you now."

He pulled back, and then plunged his cock back inside of her with one quick thrust. Velma cried out in pleasure. She wrapped her legs around his torso, and pulled him in even deeper when she did. Arching her back up to meet his deep thrusts.

I noticed they hadn't bothered with condoms, which was so unlike Velma. But then, I wasn't in a position to judge her less I was labeled a hypocrite myself.

I tried so damn hard to look away as the sound of their fucking got louder and louder. Hell, from where I was sitting, I could smell their fornication. But there was no way I couldn't watch; there was no way I couldn't deny that watching Nathan fuck my best friend wasn't getting me hot and bothered.

I felt the dampness of my black lace panties as they clung to my crotch. I spread my thighs apart, just a bit, so that my fingers could massage my clit from the other side of the material. Maybe, just maybe, this would help soothe my anger and resentment. It was worth a try.

My fingers snaked up through the elastic of my panties and found my soaked cunt as I rubbed and plied the folds of my pussy more eagerly now.

Velma was moaning loudly with each and every thrust Nathan pumped into her. She was bucking up against him. Their fucking was at an almost vicious tempo, the sound of their skin slapping against one another echoed in the still of the night. Even the crickets paused in their chirping to take notice of the intrusive noise around them.

"I'm gonna come," Thelma gasped, her voice reaching an unfamiliar pitch, "Oh God, I'm gonna come!"

"Go on then," Nathan growled, "I'm ready to shoot my load too, little girl. Let's do this!" he gritted out as he pumped into her in with a purposeful vengeance. "Aarrgghhh," he groaned loudly right before he stilled.

I knew the signs.

I'd been on the receiving end of his orgasms way more times that Velma ever would be.

I continued to thrum my clit, and pussy clenched and I came at the same time they did, but it was small compensation for what they'd done and what I'd witnessed.

Velma bucked and moaned as her orgasm released. "Oh I feel it," she rasped, "I feel your cum squirting inside of me," she bragged, and I swear to fuck, if I'd had a gun right then and there, I'd been hard pressed not to pull the trigger as I aimed it at Velma's cunt.

Nathan gave a couple of final thrusts as he emptied his seed inside of her, and then pulled his cock out, and collapsed down next to her. It took several moments for their panting to subside and their breathing to normalize.

"Fuck," she said, wiping her face with the back of her hand. "Fuck that was good."

Several minutes passed in pure silence. It was if they'd forgotten I was still there, just a few feet away, feeling ignored and devastated.

Why had I shared any of my most intimate secrets about Nathan with Velma?

I'd shared my secrets of Jeremy with her, but I had to admit, they were mostly of the PG-13 variety. Jeremy was a bore between the sheets.

Finally Nathan's deep, rich voice broke the silence. "Red, why don't you get dressed and high tail it on home now, hear? I've got to catch my breath, take a quick swim in the pond over yonder, and then try to make things up to

Prudence. We don't want her being pissed at the both of us now do we?'

"I suppose not, Nathan," she replied quietly, not looking over my way at all. She leaned over and gave him a soft kiss on his full lips and then skittered to her feet, gathering up her clothes.

As she traipsed past me she gave me a meek smile, "I'll call you tomorrow, Pru. We can make this work, I promise."

I didn't respond. I wasn't sure just what she meant by that, but she was gonna have a rude awakening if she thought for one damn minute I was going to share him.

Nathan did exactly what he said he was going to do. He took a dip in the pond, rubbing the cool water all over his body, dipping down underneath the water and then coming back up and shaking the droplets from his hair as he did.

"Wanna come join me for a swim, Pru?" he called out.

"No. I don't think so," I snapped.

He was oblivious to my anger. It was if it didn't matter; as if I didn't matter. And that hurt.

Finally, after several minutes in the pond splashing around, he came back ashore, grabbing his tee shirt to dry himself off.

"We need to come to an understanding, Pru," he said, coming over to where I was still seated in the grass, and dropping down next to me. He leaned back on his elbows, and shook more droplets of water from his hair.

"Yeah? What kind of understanding?"

"Your friend, Velma? She showed up here at nine in your place. Said you'd changed your mind and sent her to tell me. How the hell did I know different?"

"That didn't mean you needed to fuck her!" I snapped, giving him a nasty glare. "Besides that, she told me you had said ten o'clock. Obviously she had it all planned."

"Obviously she did," he said with a chuckle. "So, I fucked her. She wanted it. She made that pretty damn clear. And last time I looked, I was single, black and free to do what I want to with whoever wants me to do it. And you, you *do not* come up on me while I'm with her---or with anyone else for that matter, and bust us up like some Little Annie Oakley staking her claim, do you hear me? Because that is not happening. And that is why I had to teach you a lesson tonight, little girl."

His words to me were clear and concise. They were also said with the cold authority he evidently felt he had. And that royally pissed me off.

"Yeah, I get it," I snapped, scrambling to my feet and looking around for the shift I'd discarded.

"Now, where do you think you're going?" he asked gruffly.

"I'm getting my stuff on and going home," I snapped, "I don't like to share, sorry."

"That's because you're a spoiled little white bitch," he spat, "Go on then. I'll catch up with Red and we'll fuck all night long. She's got the stamina to match mine it would appear."

Now those words totally pissed me off. I turned back around to where he was sprawled out on the ground, and God help me if I didn't take my foot and give him a swift kick to the gut.

He didn't flinch a bit. He just laughed in his deep, rich voice which made me even madder. I drew back to give him another swift kick, but as my foot swung forward, he caught it in his tight grip, causing me to lose my balance and topple down next to him on the grass. He had hold of my leg, and my attempts to pull or twist out of his hold were pure futility.

"Got ya!" he growled. Before I could figure a way to get out of his hold, he had flipped me over onto my belly, and I was splayed across his lap.

"Let me go you fucking imbecile!" I spat. But he just continued to laugh at my lame attempts to escape his strong, firm grasp. I could feel his cock flopping around beneath my tummy as I writhed and wriggled against his lap.

"You are gonna learn a lesson, girl. And I'm just the man to teach you."

I heard the rip of my new lace panties as he tore them from me, and just as quickly, I felt the firm palm of his hand meeting the sensitive skin of my ass in a punishing slap.

"Ouch!" I squealed, trying to wriggle away. But I was going nowhere. Seconds later, another firm, open-palmed slap resounded against my ass. I jumped and wriggled again. The sting of the slap brought tears to my eyes, but he wasn't done yet. He delivered another stinging slap, and then another, until I finally figured out that the more I wriggled and squirmed, the more whacks I'd be getting.

His cock was now hard. I could feel it pressed up against my belly button. And what I also felt was the tingle in my pussy as it clenched each time his palm smacked against my butt.

"You learned your lesson yet, little girl?" he taunted with the next smack on my ass. "Tell me you won't interrupt me again like you did tonight. Tell me that and I'll quit punishing you."

I deliberately remained quiet as his hand once again landed against my butt, and I whimpered with pain and pleasure.

"You gonna be stubborn, ain't ya? That's alright, I got plenty more smacks left in me for you."

"Okay," I sobbed, "I won't interrupt you again, Nathan. I promise."

His hand landed gently on my butt, and his erection was now rock hard. He gently massaged my reddened ass. And then, I felt him raise me up as if I weighed nothing, and his lips gently grazed the skin of my throbbing buttocks.

I wiped my tears and wriggled against his mouth. He laid me on the soft grass, and changed positions so now that he was hovering over me, his erection bold and beautiful in the moonlight.

"Now that wasn't so bad, was it? I think you have learned your lesson. I think you're gonna be a good girl from now on and keep your place, aren't you?" he asked.

Before I could answer, he lowered his face to my crotch, and his tongue found my slick slit, lapping and teasing the sensitive folds. My breath hitched as the heat from his mouth and tongue kissed and licked all over my pussy.

"Mmm, baby, you taste so good," he said softly, "I didn't eat Red's pussy. Just so you know."

And for some reason, that made me feel happy knowing I was maybe a bit special to him. "But that doesn't mean I might not sometime," he finished, tongue fucking my cunt, "And you got nothing to say about it if I do."

I moaned in pleasure as he dipped a calloused finger inside of me, and wiggled it around before adding another. My pelvis bucked up against his hand, and he continued eating my pussy as if his life depended upon it.

"I need to fuck you now," he rasped, "Get on your hands and knees. I'm taking you from behind," he instructed, pulling his face from my groin.

I did as instructed, and as wet as my pussy was, Nathan had no problem guiding his dick to my slit. He took a moment, rubbing the head of it up and down to get me ready, before pushing his cockhead just inside the entrance.

"Relax your muscles, Prudence," he said, "Otherwise it's gonna hurt from this angle. You're tensed up, girl."

I made a conscious effort to relax my pelvic muscles, and he drove himself in a bit deeper.

"That's my good girl," he crooned, pushing his cock in deeper. He was right. This angle felt different being that when we usually did it this way, there was a soft mattress underneath us versus the hard ground that we were on now that had no give to it.

"Ready? I'm burying myself in you to the hilt."

And he did just that. I cried out with the first, deep thrust, but Nathan knew what he was doing. His hands were now free and he squeezed my ass cheeks together, and then started to pump into me with a rapid fury that had me gushing wetness.

"See how lubed up I got you," he groaned, as he continued pumping into me, his balls slapping against my backside in rhythm with his thrusting. "You love this cock, don't you?"

"Yesss," I mewled.

"It's yours right now, baby. You don't need to worry. When I shoot my load you know it was made just for you," he said, his hands massaging my ass and the wetness of our combined juices sounded like our own personal mating call.

I continued moaning with each of his thrusts because it felt that good. The head of his dick was rubbing against my sweet spot and I knew I'd be coming apart in a matter of seconds.

Nathan's breathing was coming hard and fast. He was gonna be right there with me. He groaned and grunted his pleasure, his hands now placed underneath, pressing against my abdomen so that his dick was hitting dead on my G-Spot and my orgasm started to unravel.

I cried out his name, and he cried out mine as he pounded into me and then suddenly stilled.

"I'm coming," he rasped. "You stay still and take it all now. Ain't gonna be no whining about you not getting yours no more, cause here it is!"

I felt the hot spurts of his jism shoot into me from his throbbing cock. My pussy clenched his dick, milking every last drop from him.

He shuddered, pumped into me a couple of more times to make sure he had emptied his balls completely. "Fucckkkk," he rasped. "You two bitches done me in tonight with those greedy white pussies."

He pulled his cock from me and rolled over onto his back. "I swear to fuck. You two have sure enough drained me," he said.

Chapter 8

July 4, 1967

Today was the annual Independence Day picnic in town. This was the last weekend before Jeremy would be getting back to town, and to be honest, I dreaded his homecoming for several reasons.

Of course, one of those reasons was because I could no longer hook up with Nathan.

Over the last month, we'd been fucking regularly. But for the last three, he'd been fucking both Velma and me. That was a fact I didn't care for at all. But there was nothing I could say about it because Nathan had certainly taught me a lesson on that one.

After that night I'd come up on them by the pond, Velma had tried like hell to call me, but I refused to talk to her. I'd simply hang up. When she stopped by the Rexall, I ignored her. It wasn't like she was going to make a scene about it in public. Her family was every bit as racist as my Daddy was, no denying that. She'd finally given up.

And I knew she was still fucking Nathan. It didn't take a rocket scientist to figure out why some nights he wasn't available to sneak into my room or to have me meet him at the pond. And I never pressed it any further because I knew his rules on that.

But the other reason; the most compelling reason I wasn't looking forward to my fiancé's return was because I was going to have to tell him the engagement was off. There was no way around it.

My period was two weeks late. I'd dropped off a urine specimen at the Planned Parenthood in the next town over two days ago. I'd called for the results. I was pregnant.

Nathan was going to be a father and I hadn't told him yet because I needed to break my engagement to Jeremy tomorrow when he got back into town. Out of respect for Jeremy, I needed to give him the bad news before I gave the good news to Nathan.

The bright spot on the horizon was that deep down I knew Nathan had wanted to get me pregnant. Why else would he have forbid condoms? Maybe now he'd toss Velma to the side and step up to his responsibilities as a soon to be father.

Today I would see Nathan at the festivities in the park. Today might be the last time I saw him before Jeremy got home. I was walking a fine timeline with the announcements, I knew. The construction on Pike Street was nearly finished. Nathan and the crew would be moving on in a few days.

I wanted to go with them. But I wasn't sure how that would work out what with them traveling from city to city.

I dressed in a new sundress I'd bought in a red, white and blue print. I brushed my hair up into a ponytail to keep my neck cool in the July heat.

Daddy was to deliver a speech today, and I knew he'd be kept busy with the meeting and greeting of the town folk, along with visitors from the rest of the county who enjoyed the day's activities of parades, picnics, and the ice cream social this evening, followed by fireworks.

I waited to head to town until around three o'clock. Nathan had said he wouldn't get there before then, and I hadn't particularly wanted to be out and about in the summer heat and humidity.

Once there, the sounds of the band playing, kids running around screaming and the street vendors chirping put me in a more festive mood. I quickly glanced around, looking for the tall, muscular hulk that was my black lover.

I walked to a different area and finally spotted him near the ice cream vendor. He saw me, nodded which was the signal that the coast was clear, and I headed around the corner and into the field leading up to the deserted boat house. Hopefully, there wouldn't be a repeat of the last time I was there with Nathan.

I snuck up, glancing around. The coast was clear. I slipped through the door and waited for him.

A few minutes later, I heard footsteps outside and Nathan slipped inside, moving an old chair up and under the door knob to make sure we weren't disturbed. My belly tingled at the sight of him.

He was wearing a white tee shirt, cutoff jean shorts and sandals. He'd bought a dish of chocolate ice cream.

"Mmm, chocolate. My favorite," I said, licking my lips.

"Yeah?" he said, "Mine too. How about if I share?"

"That'd be nice," I replied. "Sharing is good they say."

He gave me a devilish grin, my subtle message received. "Go set yourself on that couch over there," he instructed. "Pull your panties down to your ankles, and lift that pretty dress up and outta the way."

"What in the world?" I asked, quirking a brow.

"Just do it."

I complied and when I was positioned as instructed, Nathan came over and took a squatting position in front of me.

He ordered me to spread my legs and rest my feet on each of his shoulders. Once I complied, he took a spoonful of the chocolate ice cream and dropped it on my pussy. He then leaned in and licked it up. I shivered in delight.

"You're awfully horny," I commented, as he dropped another spoonful of ice cream on my crotch and proceeded to lap it up, slipping his cold tongue inside my hot pussy. I moaned this time.

"I've got some news. I'm not sure how to tell you," he said, licking his lips.

"Well, I've got some news as well. I wasn't going to say anything today, but if you're sharing your news, I might as well share mine. You go first," I said.

He dropped another spoonful of ice cream on my pussy, and this time he was achingly slow in licking it all up. He was stalling. My breath hitched. My nerves jangled.

"Velma's pregnant," he said, sitting back on his haunches and gazing up at me. "She told me this morning when we were . . . together."

So, that was the reason he couldn't meet me here until after three.

Cocksucker.

I fumbled for words. "So, how do you feel about that?" I finally asked. He thought I was going to throw a fit. But he didn't know my news yet.

"I'm happy about it. I want to father a lot of children. This will be my sixth."

What the hell?

"Uh . . . *what?*" I nearly shouted. "I thought you said you weren't married?"

He chuckled, dropping yet another spoonful of ice cream on my crotch and licking it up thoroughly.

"I'm not. Never have been," he finally replied when he'd finished licking it up. "And I won't marry. Not until I get a son that is."

"Wait? *What?*"

He sighed and sat back again. "I have five daughters spread throughout the Midwest and the South. I won't marry until I get a son."

I blinked. And then I blinked again. Words escaped me. "You . . . you don't love your girls? Any of them?" I asked incredulously.

"I send money to their mothers. But I want--I need a son to carry on my name and my legacy."

"Legacy?" I asked, clearly confused, "What exactly is your *legacy*, Nathan?"

"My legacy, Prudence, is that I fuck so damn good women will tolerate about anything I do to them, including eating sticky, chocolate ice cream out of their pussies while their daddy watches," he finished, nodding towards the one window that wasn't boarded up.

My eyes left his and immediately flew over to the window. And there he was.

My daddy.

His face was beet red with anger; his mouth pinched into a thin straight line. "You fucking white trash whore! You get your ass out of here! Go to the house pack your stuff and be on the next bus out of this town!"

He turned and walked away from the boathouse. I turned to face Nathan again.

"Who? Why?"

"Velma clued him in. Told him to be here exactly ten minutes after I walked through that door. You see, Velma knows about sharing. And she's tried to work things out with you so that we could all enjoy one another. But you? You just a spoilt ass girl of privilege who felt like taking a dark ride. She's having my baby, my son," he finished. "So I'm with her."

And with that, Nathan Crawl walked out of the boat house and out of my life. My dark lover was gone, but not without consequences.

EPILOGUE

One year later . . .

Detroit, MI

The last year has been downright brutal, but in the end, it was all worth it. Every painful bit of my struggle to make a new life for myself had paid off with the birth of my baby.

That's right. I delivered a seven pound baby boy in March. I named him Lamont Crawl Baker. He is a beautiful combination of his heritage and mine.

After I left Branchville, I took a bus to Detroit where I knew I'd be accepted. And I have been.

I quickly landed a job at General Motors before anyone knew I was pregnant. And by the time they found out, I was a member of the union and was protected against any discrimination for being single and pregnant. I got a six week maternity leave, and my hourly wage and medical benefits have allowed me to provide nicely for Lamont and me.

I have a woman in the same apartment complex who watches Lamont while I work. She's like a mother to me and a grandmother to my beautiful baby boy.

I cut off all ties, as requested, to my father. But Charlotte keeps in touch with me despite my daddy's stern orders not to do so. She sent me money until I got on my feet, and even sent a present when I had Lamont. She says he is a fine looking boy. I've sent her pictures.

Through Charlotte, I found out that Nathan stuck around Branchville after Velma was kicked out of her parents' house. Velma and Nathan rented a trailer at the mobile home park outside of town. Velma delivered a bouncing baby *girl* two weeks after Lamont was born. Charlotte said that Nathan took off before Velma was even released from the hospital.

It's funny. Both Velma and I took the same ride, but I'm the only one who held on to my dignity through it all. And I have to say that no matter how much emotional pain Nathan Crawl caused me, it was all worth it when I looked at my beautiful baby boy. Nathan gave me a gift that I would always treasure.

THE END

ABOUT THE AUTHOR

Willa Winters is a pseudonym for a best-selling author who doesn't want to horrify her friends, family and readers with the super-kink flavor of her *Scandalous Series.*

Do you enjoy lusty tales of depravity? Don't feel bad. Everyone needs to get their kink on! So, pour yourself a glass of wine, relax and take the deep dive into these scandalous books. Remember: **It's just fiction.**

SNEAK PEEKS

How about some sneak peeks of some of my other books in the Scandalous Series?

Please go to my Amazon Author Page!

Willa Winters Books

Made in the USA
Monee, IL
12 June 2024

59838346R00062